Goldilocks
and the
Three Bears

PENELOPE LIVELY

DEBI GLIORI

Hodder
Children's
Books

A division of Hodder Headline Limited

For Michael for keeps – D.G

First published in Great Britain in 1997
by Macdonald Young Books

This edition first published in 2004 by Hodder Children's Books
a division of Hodder Headline Limited
338 Euston Road London NW1 3BH

British Library Cataloguing in Publication Data
A catalogue record of this book is available from the British Library.

ISBN 0 340 87785 5 (PB)

10 9 8 7 6 5 4 3 2

Printed in China

O nce upon a time there were three
bears – a father bear, a mother bear
and a little bear.

They lived together in a house in the
woods. The house had a red roof, green
shutters and a front door with a big
brass knob.

Outside the bears' house were the tall
trees and the birds and the animals.

Inside their house there was a big bed for the father bear, a middle-sized bed for the mother bear and a small bed for the little bear.

The father's chair was a big chair, the mother's chair was a middle-sized chair and for the little bear there was a small chair.

Every morning the three bears had porridge for their breakfast. The father bear ate his porridge from a big bowl, the mother bear ate hers from a middle-sized bowl and as for the little bear, he had a special small bowl.

One day the porridge was too hot to eat, so the bears left it to cool down while they went for a walk in the woods.

A little girl called Goldilocks had also gone out for a walk in the woods that morning. She skipped along a wide track under the trees. She listened to the birds singing, she watched the squirrels and the rabbits, she picked a bunch of flowers. And then she saw a path that wound away deep into the woods, so she thought that she would see where it went.

Goldilocks followed the path and all of a sudden she found herself in front of the bears' house. As soon as she saw the red roof and the green shutters and the front door with the big brass knob she knew that she just had to go inside.

Goldilocks looked in at the window of the house. She peeked through the keyhole. Then she put her hand on the big brass knob, pushed open the door and in she went.

There on the table were three bowls of
porridge. Goldilocks took a spoon
and she helped herself to the porridge
in the big bowl – but it was much too hot.

She tried the porridge in the middle-sized bowl and that was much too cold. She took a spoonful from the small bowl and that was exactly right, so she ate it all up.

Then she sat down in the biggest chair, but it was very hard. Next she sat in the middle-sized chair, but that was too soft. So she tried the small chair, but when she sat down the chair broke to bits.

Goldilocks went upstairs to the bears' bedroom. She lay down on the big bed, but there were too many pillows. She tried the middle-sized bed, but that was lumpy. So she lay on the small bed and found that it was perfect. She covered herself up with little bear's bed cover and presently she fell fast asleep.

The three bears came back from their walk. The father bear looked at the table and then he said in his deep, gruff voice,

"WHO'S BEEN EATING MY PORRIDGE?"

The mother bear looked and she said in her soft, low voice,

"WHO'S BEEN EATING MY PORRIDGE?"

And last of all the little bear saw his bowl and he cried out in his shrill, high voice,

"WHO'S BEEN EATING MY PORRIDGE AND EATEN IT ALL UP?"

The father bear walked around the room
and when he came to the big chair he stood
stock still,

   "WHO'S BEEN SITTING IN
MY CHAIR?"

   The mother bear put down her bowl and
stared and she said,

   "WHO'S BEEN SITTING IN MY CHAIR?"

And the little bear cried out,

"WHO'S BEEN SITTING IN MY CHAIR AND
BROKEN IT ALL TO BITS?"

The three bears climbed up the stairs. The father bear opened the door to their bedroom and he said,

"WHO'S BEEN LYING IN
MY BED?"

The mother bear followed him into the room and saw that her bed was all untidy too and she said,

"WHO'S BEEN LYING IN MY BED?"

The little bear looked at his bed and he cried,

"WHO'S BEEN LYING IN MY BED AND IS
STILL THERE?"

Goldilocks was fast asleep, dreaming that she was playing in a green field on a summer's day. She didn't wake up when the father bear spoke because his voice was like thunder growling up in the sky. She just went on playing in that green field, in her dream. The mother bear didn't wake her either because her voice was like soft rain pattering on the grass and Goldilocks still went on with her dream game.

But when the little bear spoke, his voice was like the shrill, high whistling of the wind, right in Goldilocks' ear and she woke up with a start.

The dream faded away and Goldilocks knew that she was still in the bears' house, sitting up in the little bear's bed.

And then she saw the three bears. The
mother bear and the father bear were
standing on one side of the bed, looking
at her, and the little bear was at the end of
the bed and he was looking at her very
hard indeed.

Goldilocks sprang out of the bed. She rushed across the room and then she jumped clean out of the window and ran away into the woods.

Other stories to collect and treasure:

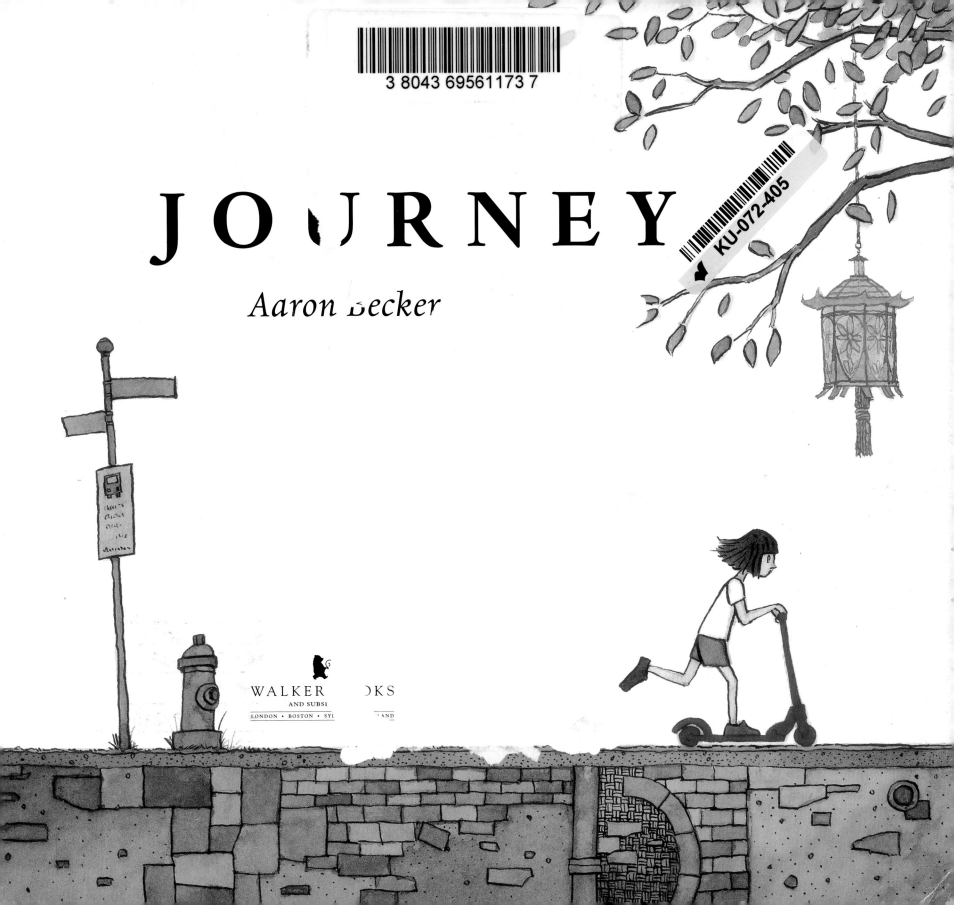

JOURNEY

Aaron Becker

WALKER   OKS
AND SUBSI
LONDON • BOSTON • SYL   AND

For Josephine

This book would not have been possible without the help of some great friends and colleagues, notably Joanne Taylor, Laurel Snyder, David Costello, Diane deGroat, Jeff Mack, Linda Pratt, Maryellen Hanley, Mary Lee Donovan and, last but not least, my wife, Darci Palmquist.

First published 2013 by Walker Books Ltd
87 Vauxhall Walk, London SE11 5HJ

This edition published 2014

10 9 8 7 6 5 4 3 2 1

© 2013 Aaron Becker

The right of Aaron Becker to be identified as author/illustrator of this work has been asserted by him in accordance with the Copyright, Designs and Patents Act 1988

Printed in China

British Library Cataloguing in Publication Data:
a catalogue record for this book is available from the British Library

ISBN 978-1-4063-5534-5

www.walker.co.uk

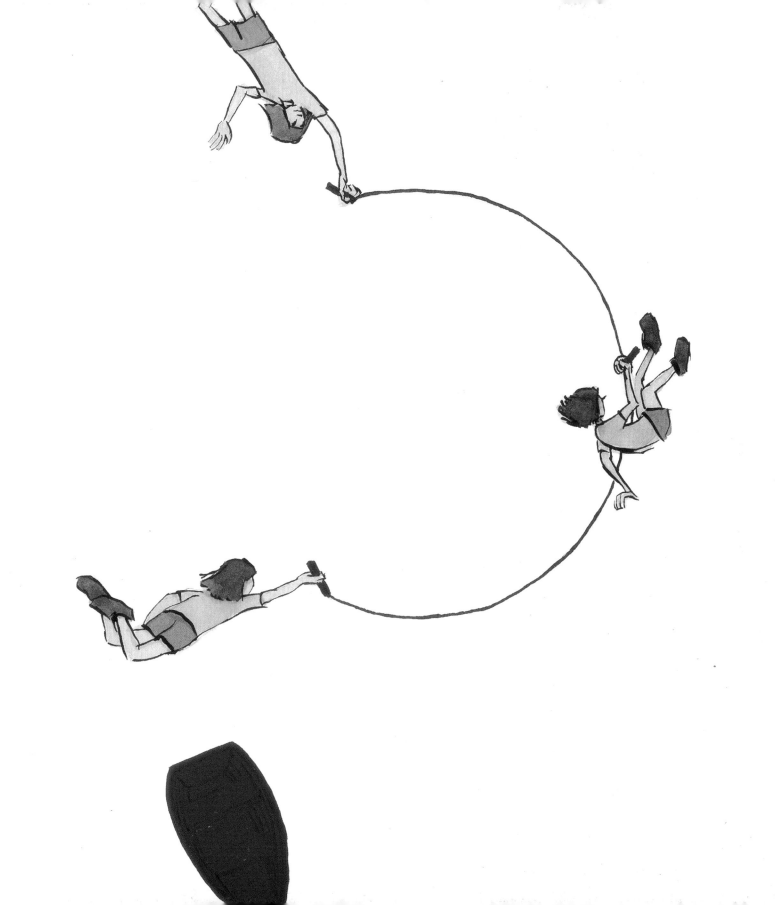

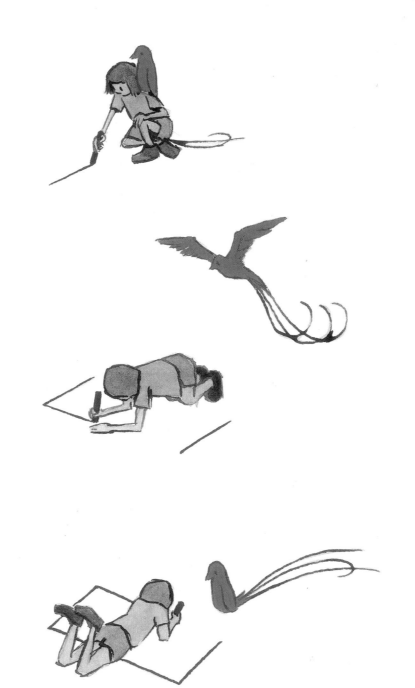